THIS WALKER
GAMEBOOK
BELONGS TO:

MY first
Story for ralle
you now

Bar be ano

First published 1998 by Walker Books Ltd
87 Vauxhall Walk, London SE11 5HJ

2 4 6 8 10 9 7 5 3 1

Text © 1998 Stella Maidment
Illustrations © 1998 Cathy Gale

This book has been typeset in
New Baskerville Educational

Printed in Hong Kong

British Library Cataloguing in Publication Data
A catalogue record for this book is available
from the British Library.

ISBN 0-7445-4494-7 (hdbk)
ISBN 0-7445-6055-1 (pbk)

To Thomas
C.G.

For Bertie
S.M.

Under this flap,
and the one on
page 23, you'll
find lots of extra
things to spot in
the big pictures.

When you have
finished reading
the story, open
out the flaps and
start searching!

Look for these things in every big picture:

Sir Percival Perfect – Sir Simply Silly's neighbour. He's always out and about doing brave and useful things, especially chasing dragons.

Something from Sir Simply Silly's washing line. He forgot the pegs one day and all his green and white clothes just blew away!

This is the story of Sir Simply Silly and his big chance to prove that he was really a brave and clever knight, not just a silly one!

Sir Simply Silly had never done anything bold and daring before. He got into some tricky situations and had to solve a lot of puzzles along the way.

Can you help Sir Simply Silly?

- **Read the story and solve the puzzles.**

- **Check your answers at the back when you reach the end, or if you get really stuck.**

A BRAVE KNIGHT TO THE RESCUE!

Stella Maidment

illustrated by

Cathy Gale

WALKER BOOKS
AND SUBSIDIARIES
LONDON · BOSTON · SYDNEY

This is Sir Simply Silly.
He often gets things wrong
so he'll need your help!

Sir Simply Silly wished that he could be a proper knight just like his neighbour, Sir Percival Perfect.

Sir Percival was clever and brave. He was always being sent on special missions by the king.

The king **had** smiled at Sir Simply Silly once but only because a bit of his armour had just fallen off.

That was the way Sir Simply Silly was – he couldn't get anything right. Even his castle was a silly place!

 Can you spot six silly things that he has done in the castle?

Could you help me

One day Sir Simply Silly was out in the woods hoping to meet a dragon ...

when a piece of paper fluttered down and landed right in front of him.

"It's part of a message," gasped Sir Simply Silly. "An urgent message for ME!"

"I wonder where the other pieces are?" he thought. "I'll look around and see if I can find them."

 Can you find six more pieces? Who was the message really for?

Dear Sir Percival Perfect

Only you can help us!
We are prisoners in the
giant's Great Tower.
Please come quickly.
Fergus and Fenella

Sir Simply Silly didn't find
the first part of the message.
But he found all the rest...

"Gosh!" gasped Sir Simply
Silly. "A real quest at last! A
dangerous mission for me!
My big chance!"

"Here I come," he said. "A brave knight to the rescue!" But he had a feeling he'd forgotten something.

"Oh, silly me!" he said. "I'll need to find my horse. Now where is she?"

All the horses have a twin – except one. Can you find the five pairs of twins? The odd one out is Sir Simply Silly's little horse!

So Sir Simply Silly saddled his horse and rode off in search of the giant's castle.

The only trouble was ... he didn't know which way to go! Luckily he met a wise old woman at the crossroads.

"Just follow this path," she said. "But whatever you do, don't go over the red bridge."

A little later Sir Simply Silly stopped and frowned. "Now what was it she said? Ah yes – go over the red bridge."

And so he went the silly way! How did he get to the giant's castle? Which way should he have gone?

But when he reached the giant's castle there were two fierce guards at the door.

"My goodness," said Sir Simply Silly. "You must be twins. You're both exactly the same."

"We're brothers, not twins," said one of the guards. "Any fool can see there are five differences between us."

"Wrong!" said the other. "There are SIX differences between us, stupid."
"It's FIVE," shouted the first, and they began to fight.

Who was right? Are there five or six differences between the guards?

While the guards were arguing Sir Simply Silly crept through the door.

Luckily the giant was asleep. His keys were lying on the floor near by.

Sir Simply Silly had no idea which key would open the Great Tower.

So he just picked his favourite colour – green!

Which key had the green label? Follow the string to find out. Now look at the castle plan. Do you think he made a good choice?

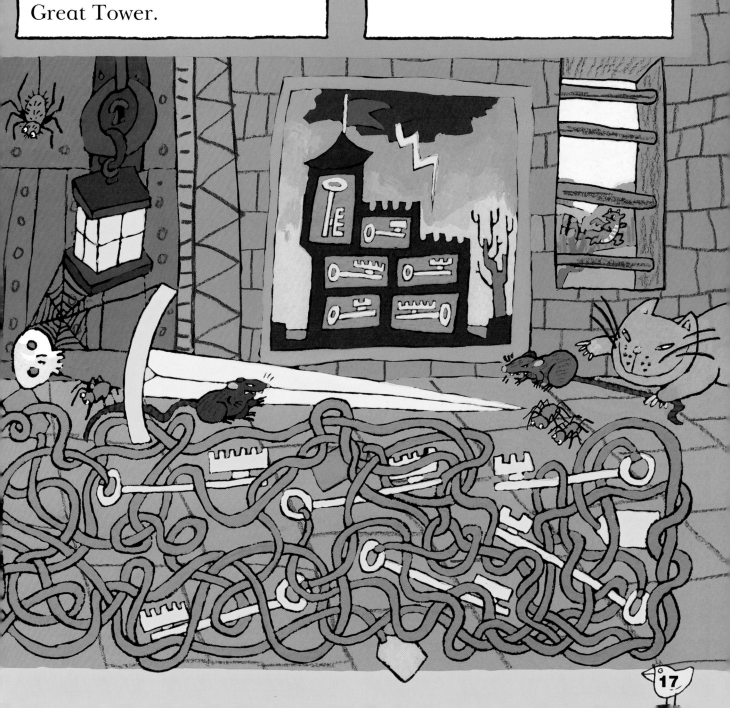

He climbed the giant stairs and pushed the key into the lock. It turned! And the door swung open.

Sir Simply Silly fell inside! The two prisoners jumped up. "Sir Percival!" they cried. "We knew you'd rescue us!"

"Actually it's me," explained Sir Simply Silly as they all rushed out of the room.

But the giant had woken up. He was coming up the stairs! A door led out on to the battlements. But could they escape?

Can you help them find a safe way down?

"What fun!" said Sir Simply Silly. "I love slides."

A huge roar came from the Great Tower – the giant had realized they were gone!

"We can't all escape on your horse!" said Fenella. "What are we going to do?"

At that moment some carts came rattling by, on their way to the palace from the royal farm. Sir Simply Silly had an idea...

Where are they hiding? Look carefully. You may be able to see their feet!

When the carts stopped at the palace the children jumped out. "We're home! We're home!" they cried.

Sir Simply Silly was amazed. "You mean you're the king's children," he gasped. "Prince Fergus and Princess Fenella?"

Under this flap, and the one on page 4, you'll find lots of extra things to spot in the big pictures.

When you have finished reading the story, open out the flaps and start searching!

Look for these things in every big picture:

Sir Simply Silly's four dogs. They like to follow him about but they aren't in every picture – you'll find each dog just once.

The Silly family sword. Sir Simply Silly lost it some time ago. You'll see it just once.

Sir Simply Silly was a hero! That night the king held a banquet especially for him, and all the food was GREEN!

One of the shields has pictures from the story – a bird, a horse, a key and the Great Tower. Can you see which one?

Goodbye and thank you for your help!

23

The Answers

- The answers to the story puzzles are shown with single black lines.

- The answers to the fun flap puzzles are shown with double black lines.

Pages 6 and 7

Pages 4 and 5

Pages 8 and 9

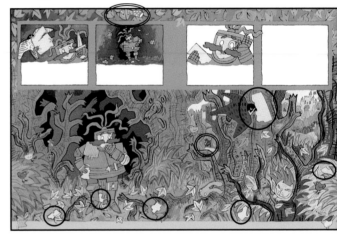

The message was really for Sir Percival Perfect.

Pages 10 and 11

Pages 12 and 13

Pages 14 and 15

There are five differences between the guards.

Pages 16 and 17

Pages 18 and 19

Pages 20 and 21

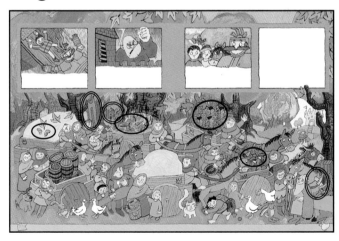

Pages 22 and 23

25

MORE WALKER PAPERBACKS
For You to Enjoy

Some Skill Level 1 Gamebooks

GHOST HUNT AT TREMBLY TOWERS
by Molly Williams/Chris Fisher

A hair-raising haunted-house puzzle adventure.

0-7445-6051-9   £4.99

HORNPIPE'S HUNT FOR PIRATE GOLD
by Marjorie Newman/Ben Cort

A swashbuckling pirate puzzle adventure.

0-7445-6053-5   £4.99

A BRAVE KNIGHT TO THE RESCUE!
by Stella Maidment/Cathy Gale

A thrilling knight puzzle quest.

0-7445-6055-1   £4.99

SPACE CHASE ON PLANET ZOG
by Karen King/Alan Rowe

A zappy space puzzle adventure.

0-7445-6050-0   £4.99

MYSTERY OF THE MONSTER PARTY
by Deri Robins/Anni Axworthy

A monstrous puzzle adventure.

0-7445-6054-3   £4.99

THE WONDERFUL JOURNEY OF CAMERON CAT
by Marjorie Newman/Charlotte Hard

An entertaining cat puzzle adventure.

0-7445-6052-7   £4.99

Walker Paperbacks are available from most booksellers, or by post from B.B.C.S., P.O. Box 941, Hull, North Humberside HU1 3YQ

24 hour telephone credit card line 01482 224626

To order, send: Title, author, ISBN number and price for each book ordered, your full name and address,
cheque or postal order payable to BBCS for the total amount and allow the following for postage and packing:
UK and BFPO: £1.00 for the first book, and 50p for each additional book to a maximum of £3.50.
Overseas and Eire: £2.00 for the first book, £1.00 for the second and 50p for each additional book.

Prices and availability are subject to change without notice.